I0684614

Sketches of Young Couples

Charles Dickens

Contents

SKETCHES OF YOUNG COUPLES

BY

Charles Dickens

SKETCHES OF YOUNG COUPLES

AN URGENT REMONSTRANCE, &c

TO THE GENTLEMEN OF ENGLAND,

(BEING BACHELORS OR WIDOWERS,)

THE REMONSTRANCE OF THEIR FAITHFUL FELLOW-SUBJECT,

SHEWETH,-

THAT Her Most Gracious Majesty, Victoria, by the Grace of God of the United Kingdom of Great Britain and Ireland Queen, Defender of the Faith, did, on the 23rd day of November last past, declare and pronounce to Her Most Honourable Privy Council, Her Majesty's Most Gracious intention of entering into the bonds of wedlock.

THAT Her Most Gracious Majesty, in so making known Her Most Gracious intention to Her Most Honourable Privy Council as aforesaid, did use and employ the words--'It is my intention to ally myself in marriage with Prince Albert of Saxe Coburg and Gotha.'

THAT the present is Bissextile, or Leap Year, in which it is held and considered lawful for any lady to offer and submit proposals of marriage to any gentleman, and to enforce and insist upon acceptance of the same, under pain of a certain fine or penalty; to wit, one silk or satin dress of the first quality, to be chosen by the lady and paid (or owed) for, by the gentleman.

THAT these and other the horrors and dangers with which the said Bissextile, or Leap Year, threatens the gentlemen of England on every occasion of its periodical return, have been greatly aggravated and augmented by the terms of Her Majesty's said Most Gracious communication, which have filled the heads of divers young ladies in this Realm with certain new ideas destructive to the peace of mankind, that never entered their imagination before.

THAT a case has occurred in Camberwell, in which a young lady informed her Papa that 'she intended to ally herself in marriage' with Mr. Smith of Stepney; and that another, and a very distressing case, has occurred at Tottenham, in which a young lady not only stated her intention of allying herself in marriage with her cousin John, but, taking violent possession of her said cousin, actually married him.

THAT similar outrages are of constant occurrence, not only in the capital and its neighbourhood, but throughout the kingdom, and that unless the excited female populace be speedily checked and restrained in their lawless proceedings, most deplorable results must ensue therefrom; among which may be anticipated a most alarming increase in the population of the country, with which no efforts of the agricultural or manufacturing interest can possibly keep pace.

THAT there is strong reason to suspect the existence of a most extensive plot, conspiracy, or design, secretly contrived by vast numbers of single ladies in the United Kingdom of Great Britain and Ireland, and now extending its ramifications in every quarter of the land; the object and intent of which plainly appears to be the holding and solemnising of an enormous and unprecedented number of marriages, on the day on which the nuptials of Her said Most Gracious Majesty are performed.

THAT such plot, conspiracy, or design, strongly savours of Popery, as tending to the discomfiture of the Clergy of the Established Church, by entailing upon them great mental and physical exhaustion; and that such Popish plots are fomented and encouraged by Her Majesty's Ministers, which clearly appears--not only from Her Majesty's principal Secretary of State for Foreign Affairs traitorously getting married while holding office under the Crown; but from Mr. O'Connell having been heard to declare and avow that, if he had a daughter to marry, she should be married on the same day as Her said Most Gracious Majesty.

THAT such arch plots, conspiracies, and designs, besides being fraught with danger to the Established Church, and (consequently) to the State, cannot fail to bring ruin and bankruptcy upon a large class of Her Majesty's subjects; as a great and sudden increase in the number of married men occasioning the comparative desertion (for a time) of Taverns, Hotels, Billiard-rooms, and Gaming-Houses, will deprive the Proprietors of their accustomed profits and returns. And in further proof of the depth and baseness of such designs, it may be here observed, that all proprietors of Taverns, Hotels, Billiard-rooms, and Gaming-Houses, are (especially the last) solemnly devoted to the Protestant religion.

FOR all these reasons, and many others of no less gravity and import, an urgent appeal is made to the gentlemen of England (being bachelors or widowers) to take immediate steps for convening a Public meeting; To consider of the best and surest means of averting the dangers with which they are threatened by the recurrence of Bissextile, or Leap Year, and the additional sensation created among single ladies by the terms of Her Majesty's Most Gracious Declaration; To take measures, without delay, for resisting the said single Ladies, and counteracting their evil designs; And to pray Her Majesty to dismiss her present Ministers, and to summon to her Councils those distinguished Gentlemen in various Honourable Professions who, by insulting on all occasions the only Lady in England who can be insulted with safety, have given a sufficient guarantee to Her Majesty's Loving Subjects that they, at least, are qualified to make war with women, and are already expert in the use of those weapons which are common to the lowest and most abandoned of the sex.

THE YOUNG COUPLE

There is to be a wedding this morning at the corner house in the terrace. The pastry-cook's people have been there half-a-dozen times already; all day yesterday there was a great stir and bustle, and they were up this morning as soon as it was light. Miss Emma Fielding is going to be married to young Mr. Harvey.

Heaven alone can tell in what bright colours this marriage is painted upon the mind of the little housemaid at number six, who has hardly slept a wink all night with thinking of it, and now stands on the unswept door-steps leaning upon her

broom, and looking wistfully towards the enchanted house. Nothing short of om-
niscience can divine what visions of the baker, or the green- grocer, or the smart
and most insinuating butterman, are flitting across her mind--what thoughts of
how she would dress on such an occasion, if she were a lady--of how she would
dress, if she were only a bride--of how cook would dress, being bridesmaid, con-
jointly with her sister 'in place' at Fulham, and how the clergyman, deeming them
so many ladies, would be quite humbled and respectful. What day-dreams of hope
and happiness--of life being one perpetual holiday, with no master and no mistress
to grant or withhold it--of every Sunday being a Sunday out--of pure freedom as to
curls and ringlets, and no obligation to hide fine heads of hair in caps-- what pictures of happiness, vast and immense to her, but utterly ridiculous to us, bewilder
the brain of the little housemaid at number six, all called into existence by the wedding at the corner!

   We smile at such things, and so we should, though perhaps for a better reason than commonly presents itself. It should be pleasant to us to know that there
are notions of happiness so moderate and limited, since upon those who entertain
them, happiness and lightness of heart are very easily bestowed.

   But the little housemaid is awakened from her reverie, for forth from the door
of the magical corner house there runs towards her, all fluttering in smart new
dress and streaming ribands, her friend Jane Adams, who comes all out of breath to
redeem a solemn promise of taking her in, under cover of the confusion, to see the
breakfast table spread forth in state, and--sight of sights!--her young mistress ready
dressed for church.

   And there, in good truth, when they have stolen up-stairs on tip- toe and edged
themselves in at the chamber-door--there is Miss Emma 'looking like the sweetest
picter,' in a white chip bonnet and orange flowers, and all other elegancies becoming a bride, (with the make, shape, and quality of every article of which the girl is
perfectly familiar in one moment, and never forgets to her dying day)--and there
is Miss Emma's mamma in tears, and Miss Emma's papa comforting her, and saying
how that of course she has been long looking forward to this, and how happy she
ought to be--and there too is Miss Emma's sister with her arms round her neck,
and the other bridesmaid all smiles and tears, quieting the children, who would cry
more but that they are so finely dressed, and yet sob for fear sister Emma should be

taken away--and it is all so affecting, that the two servant-girls cry more than any-body; and Jane Adams, sitting down upon the stairs, when they have crept away, declares that her legs tremble so that she don't know what to do, and that she will say for Miss Emma, that she never had a hasty word from her, and that she does hope and pray she may be happy.

But Jane soon comes round again, and then surely there never was anything like the breakfast table, glittering with plate and china, and set out with flowers and sweets, and long-necked bottles, in the most sumptuous and dazzling manner. In the centre, too, is the mighty charm, the cake, glistening with frosted sugar, and garnished beautifully. They agree that there ought to be a little Cupid under one of the barley-sugar temples, or at least two hearts and an arrow; but, with this ex-ception, there is nothing to wish for, and a table could not be handsomer. As they arrive at this conclusion, who should come in but Mr. John! to whom Jane says that its only Anne from number six; and John says HE knows, for he's often winked his eye down the area, which causes Anne to blush and look confused. She is going away, indeed; when Mr. John will have it that she must drink a glass of wine, and he says never mind it's being early in the morning, it won't hurt her: so they shut the door and pour out the wine; and Anne drinking lane's health, and adding, 'and here's wishing you yours, Mr. John,' drinks it in a great many sips,--Mr. John all the time making jokes appropriate to the occasion. At last Mr. John, who has waxed bolder by degrees, pleads the usage at weddings, and claims the privilege of a kiss, which he obtains after a great scuffle; and footsteps being now heard on the stairs, they disperse suddenly.

By this time a carriage has driven up to convey the bride to church, and Anne of number six prolonging the process of 'cleaning her door,' has the satisfaction of beholding the bride and bridesmaids, and the papa and mamma, hurry into the same and drive rapidly off. Nor is this all, for soon other carriages begin to arrive with a posse of company all beautifully dressed, at whom she could stand and gaze for ever; but having something else to do, is compelled to take one last long look and shut the street-door.

And now the company have gone down to breakfast, and tears have given place to smiles, for all the corks are out of the long-necked bottles, and their contents are disappearing rapidly. Miss Emma's papa is at the top of the table; Miss Emma's

mamma at the bottom; and beside the latter are Miss Emma herself and her husband,-- admitted on all hands to be the handsomest and most interesting young
couple ever known. All down both sides of the table, too, are various young ladies,
beautiful to see, and various young gentlemen who seem to think so; and there, in a
post of honour, is an unmarried aunt of Miss Emma's, reported to possess unheard-of
riches, and to have expressed vast testamentary intentions respecting her favourite
niece and new nephew. This lady has been very liberal and generous already, as the
jewels worn by the bride abundantly testify, but that is nothing to what she means
to do, or even to what she has done, for she put herself in close communication with
the dressmaker three months ago, and prepared a wardrobe (with some articles
worked by her own hands) fit for a Princess. People may call her an old maid, and
so she may be, but she is neither cross nor ugly for all that; on the contrary, she is
very cheerful and pleasant-looking, and very kind and tender- hearted: which is no
matter of surprise except to those who yield to popular prejudices without thinking
why, and will never grow wiser and never know better.

   Of all the company though, none are more pleasant to behold or better pleased
with themselves than two young children, who, in honour of the day, have seats
among the guests. Of these, one is a little fellow of six or eight years old, brother
to the bride,--and the other a girl of the same age, or something younger, whom he
calls 'his wife.' The real bride and bridegroom are not more devoted than they: he
all love and attention, and she all blushes and fondness, toying with a little bouquet
which he gave her this morning, and placing the scattered rose-leaves in her bosom
with nature's own coquettishness. They have dreamt of each other in their quiet
dreams, these children, and their little hearts have been nearly broken when the
absent one has been dispraised in jest. When will there come in after-life a passion
so earnest, generous, and true as theirs; what, even in its gentlest realities, can have
the grace and charm that hover round such fairy lovers!

   By this time the merriment and happiness of the feast have gained their height;
certain ominous looks begin to be exchanged between the bridesmaids, and some-
how it gets whispered about that the carriage which is to take the young couple
into the country has arrived. Such members of the party as are most disposed to
prolong its enjoyments, affect to consider this a false alarm, but it turns out too true,
being speedily confirmed, first by the retirement of the bride and a select file of in-

timates who are to prepare her for the journey, and secondly by the withdrawal of the ladies generally. To this there ensues a particularly awkward pause, in which everybody essays to be facetious, and nobody succeeds; at length the bridegroom makes a mysterious disappearance in obedience to some equally mysterious signal; and the table is deserted.

Now, for at least six weeks last past it has been solemnly devised and settled that the young couple should go away in secret; but they no sooner appear without the door than the drawing-room windows are blocked up with ladies waving their handkerchiefs and kissing their hands, and the dining-room panes with gentlemen's faces beaming farewell in every queer variety of its expression. The hall and steps are crowded with servants in white favours, mixed up with particular friends and relations who have darted out to say good-bye; and foremost in the group are the tiny lovers arm in arm, thinking, with fluttering hearts, what happiness it would be to dash away together in that gallant coach, and never part again.

The bride has barely time for one hurried glance at her old home, when the steps rattle, the door slams, the horses clatter on the pavement, and they have left it far away.

A knot of women servants still remain clustered in the hall, whispering among themselves, and there of course is Anne from number six, who has made another escape on some plea or other, and been an admiring witness of the departure. There are two points on which Anne expatiates over and over again, without the smallest appearance of fatigue or intending to leave off; one is, that she 'never see in all her life such a--oh such a angel of a gentleman as Mr. Harvey'--and the other, that she 'can't tell how it is, but it don't seem a bit like a work-a-day, or a Sunday neither--it's all so unsettled and unregular.'

THE FORMAL COUPLE

The formal couple are the most prim, cold, immovable, and unsatisfactory people on the face of the earth. Their faces, voices, dress, house, furniture, walk, and manner, are all the essence of formality, unrelieved by one redeeming touch of frankness, heartiness, or nature.

Everything with the formal couple resolves itself into a matter of form. They don't call upon you on your account, but their own; not to see how you are, but to show how they are: it is not a ceremony to do honour to you, but to themselves,-- not due to your position, but to theirs. If one of a friend's children die, the formal couple are as sure and punctual in sending to the house as the undertaker; if a friend's family be increased, the monthly nurse is not more attentive than they. The formal couple, in fact, joyfully seize all occasions of testifying their good-breeding and precise observance of the little usages of society; and for you, who are the means to this end, they care as much as a man does for the tailor who has enabled him to cut a figure, or a woman for the milliner who has assisted her to a conquest.

Having an extensive connexion among that kind of people who make acquaintances and eschew friends, the formal gentleman attends from time to time a great many funerals, to which he is formally invited, and to which he formally goes, as returning a call for the last time. Here his deportment is of the most faultless description; he knows the exact pitch of voice it is proper to assume, the sombre look he ought to wear, the melancholy tread which should be his gait for the day. He is perfectly acquainted with all the dreary courtesies to be observed in a mourning-coach; knows when to sigh, and when to hide his nose in the white handkerchief; and looks into the grave and shakes his head when the ceremony is concluded, with the sad formality of a mute.

'What kind of funeral was it?' says the formal lady, when he returns home. 'Oh!' replies the formal gentleman, 'there never was such a gross and disgusting impropriety; there were no feathers.' 'No feathers!' cries the lady, as if on wings of black feathers dead people fly to Heaven, and, lacking them, they must of necessity go elsewhere. Her husband shakes his head; and further adds, that they had seed-cake instead of plum-cake, and that it was all white wine. 'All white wine!' exclaims his wife. 'Nothing but sherry and madeira,' says the husband. 'What! no port?' 'Not a drop.' No port, no plums, and no feathers! 'You will recollect, my dear,' says the formal lady, in a voice of stately reproof, 'that when we first met this poor man who is now dead and gone, and he took that very strange course of addressing me at dinner without being previously introduced, I ventured to express my opinion that the family were quite ignorant of etiquette, and very imperfectly acquainted with the decencies of life. You have now had a good opportunity of judging for yourself, and all I have to say is, that I trust you will never go to a funeral THERE again.' 'My dear,' replies the formal gentleman, 'I never will.' So the informal deceased is cut in his grave; and the formal couple, when they tell the story of the funeral, shake their heads, and wonder what some people's feelings ARE made of, and what their notions of propriety CAN be!

If the formal couple have a family (which they sometimes have), they are not children, but little, pale, sour, sharp-nosed men and women; and so exquisitely brought up, that they might be very old dwarfs for anything that appeareth to the contrary. Indeed, they are so acquainted with forms and conventionalities, and conduct themselves with such strict decorum, that to see the little girl break a look-ing-glass in some wild outbreak, or the little boy kick his parents, would be to any visitor an unspeakable relief and consolation.

The formal couple are always sticklers for what is rigidly proper, and have a great readiness in detecting hidden impropriety of speech or thought, which by less scrupulous people would be wholly unsuspected. Thus, if they pay a visit to the theatre, they sit all night in a perfect agony lest anything improper or immoral should proceed from the stage; and if anything should happen to be said which admits of a double construction, they never fail to take it up directly, and to express by their looks the great outrage which their feelings have sustained. Perhaps this is their chief reason for absenting themselves almost entirely from places of public amusement. They go sometimes to the Exhibition of the Royal Academy;--but that is often more shocking than the stage itself, and the formal lady thinks that it really is high time Mr. Etty was prosecuted and made a public example of.

We made one at a christening party not long since, where there were amongst the guests a formal couple, who suffered the acutest torture from certain jokes, incidental to such an occasion, cut-- and very likely dried also--by one of the godfathers; a red-faced elderly gentleman, who, being highly popular with the rest of the company, had it all his own way, and was in great spirits. It was at supper-time that this gentleman came out in full force. We-- being of a grave and quiet demeanour--had been chosen to escort the formal lady down-stairs, and, sitting beside her, had a favourable opportunity of observing her emotions.

We have a shrewd suspicion that, in the very beginning, and in the first blush--literally the first blush--of the matter, the formal lady had not felt quite certain whether the being present at such a ceremony, and encouraging, as it were, the public exhibition of a baby, was not an act involving some degree of indelicacy and impropriety; but certain we are that when that baby's health was drunk, and allusions were made, by a grey-headed gentleman proposing it, to the time when he had dandled in his arms the young Christian's mother,--certain we are that then the formal lady took the alarm, and recoiled from the old gentleman as from a hoary profligate. Still she bore it; she fanned herself with an indignant air, but still she bore it. A comic song was sung, involving a confession from some imaginary gentleman that he had kissed a female, and yet the formal lady bore it. But when at last, the health of the godfather before-mentioned being drunk, the godfather rose to return thanks, and in the course of his observations darkly hinted at babies yet unborn, and even contemplated the possibility of the subject of that festival having brothers and sisters, the formal lady could endure no more, but, bowing slightly round, and sweeping haughtily past the offender, left the room in tears, under the protection of the formal gentleman.

THE LOVING COUPLE

There cannot be a better practical illustration of the wise saw and ancient instance, that there may be too much of a good thing, than is presented by a loving couple. Undoubtedly it is meet and proper that two persons joined together in holy matrimony should be loving, and unquestionably it is pleasant to know and see that they are so; but there is a time for all things, and the couple who happen to be always in a loving state before company, are well-nigh intolerable.

And in taking up this position we would have it distinctly understood that we do not seek alone the sympathy of bachelors, in whose objection to loving couples we recognise interested motives and personal considerations. We grant that to that unfortunate class of society there may be something very irritating, tantalising, and provoking, in being compelled to witness those gentle endearments and chaste interchanges which to loving couples are quite the ordinary business of life. But while we recognise the natural character of the prejudice to which these unhappy men are subject, we can neither receive their biassed evidence, nor address ourself to their inflamed and angered minds. Dispassionate experience is our only guide; and in these moral essays we seek no less to reform hymeneal offenders than to hold out a timely warning to all rising couples, and even to those who have not yet set forth upon their pilgrimage towards the matrimonial market.

Let all couples, present or to come, therefore profit by the example of Mr. and Mrs. Leaver, themselves a loving couple in the first degree.

Mr. and Mrs. Leaver are pronounced by Mrs. Starling, a widow lady who lost her husband when she was young, and lost herself about the same-time--for by her own count she has never since grown five years older--to be a perfect model of wedded felicity. 'You would suppose,' says the romantic lady, 'that they were lovers only just now engaged. Never was such happiness! They are so tender, so affectionate, so attached to each other, so enamoured, that positively nothing can be more charming!'

'Augusta, my soul,' says Mr. Leaver. 'Augustus, my life,' replies Mrs. Leaver. 'Sing some little ballad, darling,' quoth Mr. Leaver. 'I couldn't, indeed, dearest,' returns Mrs. Leaver. 'Do, my dove,' says Mr. Leaver. 'I couldn't possibly, my love,' replies Mrs. Leaver; 'and it's very naughty of you to ask me.' 'Naughty, darling!' cries Mr. Leaver. 'Yes, very naughty, and very cruel,' returns Mrs. Leaver, 'for you know I have a sore throat, and that to sing would give me great pain. You're a monster, and I hate you. Go away!' Mrs. Leaver has said 'go away,' because Mr. Leaver has tapped her under the chin: Mr. Leaver not doing as he is bid, but on the contrary, sitting down beside her, Mrs. Leaver slaps Mr. Leaver; and Mr. Leaver in return slaps Mrs. Leaver, and it being now time for all persons present to look the other way, they look the other way, and hear a still small sound as of kissing, at which Mrs. Starling is thoroughly enraptured, and whispers her neighbour that if all married couples were like that, what a heaven this earth would be!

The loving couple are at home when this occurs, and maybe only three or four friends are present, but, unaccustomed to reserve upon this interesting point, they are pretty much the same abroad. Indeed upon some occasions, such as a pic-nic or a water-party, their lovingness is even more developed, as we had an opportunity last summer of observing in person.

There was a great water-party made up to go to Twickenham and dine, and afterwards dance in an empty villa by the river-side, hired expressly for the purpose.

Mr. and Mrs. Leaver were of the company; and it was our fortune to have a seat in the same boat, which was an eight-oared galley, manned by amateurs, with a blue striped awning of the same pattern as their Guernsey shirts, and a dingy red flag of the same shade as the whiskers of the stroke oar. A coxswain being appointed, and all other matters adjusted, the eight gentlemen threw themselves into strong paroxysms, and pulled up with the tide, stimulated by the compassionate remarks of the ladies, who one and all exclaimed, that it seemed an immense exertion--as indeed it did. At first we raced the other boat, which came alongside in gallant style; but this being found an unpleasant amusement, as giving rise to a great quantity of splashing, and rendering the cold pies and other viands very moist, it was unanimously voted down, and we were suffered to shoot a- head, while the second boat followed ingloriously in our wake.

It was at this time that we first recognised Mr. Leaver. There were two firemen-watermen in the boat, lying by until somebody was exhausted; and one of them, who had taken upon himself the direction of affairs, was heard to cry in a gruff voice, 'Pull away, number two--give it her, number two--take a longer reach, number two--now, number two, sir, think you're winning a boat.' The greater part of the company had no doubt begun to wonder which of the striped Guernseys it might be that stood in need of such encouragement, when a stifled shriek from Mrs. Leaver confirmed the doubtful and informed the ignorant; and Mr. Leaver, still further disguised in a straw hat and no neckcloth, was observed to be in a fearful perspiration, and failing visibly. Nor was the general consternation diminished at this instant by the same gentleman (in the performance of an accidental aquatic feat, termed 'catching a crab') plunging suddenly backward, and displaying nothing of himself to the company, but two violently struggling legs. Mrs. Leaver shrieked again several times, and cried piteously--'Is he dead? Tell me the worst. Is he dead?'

Now, a moment's reflection might have convinced the loving wife, that unless her husband were endowed with some most surprising powers of muscular action, he never could be dead while he kicked so hard; but still Mrs. Leaver cried, 'Is he dead? is he dead?' and still everybody else cried--'No, no, no,' until such time as Mr. Leaver was replaced in a sitting posture, and his oar (which had been going through all kinds of wrong-headed performances on its own account) was once more put in his hand, by the exertions of the two firemen-watermen. Mr. Leaver then exclaimed, 'Augustus, my child, come to me;' and Mr. Leaver said, 'Augusta, my love, compose yourself, I am not injured.' But Mrs. Leaver cried again more piteously than before, 'Augustus, my child, come to me;' and now the company generally, who seemed to be apprehensive that if Mr. Leaver remained where he was, he might contribute more than his proper share towards the drowning of the party, disinterestedly took part with Mrs. Leaver, and said he really ought to go, and that he was not strong enough for such violent exercise, and ought never to have undertaken it. Reluctantly, Mr. Leaver went, and laid himself down at Mrs. Leaver's feet, and Mrs. Leaver stooping over him, said, 'Oh Augustus, how could you terrify me so?' and Mr. Leaver said, 'Augusta, my sweet, I never meant to terrify you;' and Mrs. Leaver said, 'You are faint, my dear;' and Mr. Leaver said, 'I am rather so, my love;' and they were very loving indeed under Mrs. Leaver's veil, until at length Mr. Leaver came forth again, and pleasantly asked if he had not heard something said about bottled stout and sandwiches.

Mrs. Starling, who was one of the party, was perfectly delighted with this scene, and frequently murmured half-aside, 'What a loving couple you are!' or 'How delightful it is to see man and wife so happy together!' To us she was quite poetical, (for we are a kind of cousins,) observing that hearts beating in unison like that made life a paradise of sweets; and that when kindred creatures were drawn together by sympathies so fine and delicate, what more than mortal happiness did not our souls partake! To all this we answered 'Certainly,' or 'Very true,' or merely sighed, as the case might be. At every new act of the loving couple, the widow's admiration broke out afresh; and when Mrs. Leaver would not permit Mr. Leaver to keep his hat off, lest the sun should strike to his head, and give him a brain fever, Mrs. Starling actually shed tears, and said it reminded her of Adam and Eve.

The loving couple were thus loving all the way to Twickenham, but when we arrived there (by which time the amateur crew looked very thirsty and vicious) they were more playful than ever, for Mrs. Leaver threw stones at Mr. Leaver, and Mr. Leaver ran after Mrs. Leaver on the grass, in a most innocent and enchanting manner. At dinner, too, Mr. Leaver WOULD steal Mrs. Leaver's tongue, and Mrs. Leaver WOULD retaliate upon Mr. Leaver's fowl; and when Mrs. Leaver was going to take some lobster salad, Mr. Leaver wouldn't let her have any, saying that it made her ill, and she was always sorry for it afterwards, which afforded Mrs. Leaver an opportunity of pretending to be cross, and showing many other prettinesses. But this was merely the smiling surface of their loves, not the mighty depths of the stream, down to which the company, to say the truth, dived rather unexpectedly, from the following accident. It chanced that Mr. Leaver took upon himself to propose the bachelors who had first originated the notion of that entertainment, in doing which, he affected to regret that he was no longer of their body himself, and pretended grievously to lament his fallen state. This Mrs. Leaver's feelings could not brook, even in jest, and consequently, exclaiming aloud, 'He loves me not, he loves me not!' she fell in a very pitiable state into the arms of Mrs. Starling, and, directly becoming insensible, was conveyed by that lady and her husband into another room. Presently Mr. Leaver came running back to know if there was a medical gentleman in company, and as there was, (in what company is there not?) both Mr. Leaver and the medical gentleman hurried away together.

The medical gentleman was the first who returned, and among his intimate friends he was observed to laugh and wink, and look as unmedical as might be; but when Mr. Leaver came back he was very solemn, and in answer to all inquiries, shook his head, and remarked that Augusta was far too sensitive to be trifled with--an opinion which the widow subsequently confirmed. Finding that she was in no imminent peril, however, the rest of the party betook themselves to dancing on the green, and very merry and happy they were, and a vast quantity of flirtation there was; the last circumstance being no doubt attributable, partly to the fineness of the weather, and partly to the locality, which is well known to be favourable to all harmless recreations.

In the bustle of the scene, Mr. and Mrs. Leaver stole down to the boat, and disposed themselves under the awning, Mrs. Leaver reclining her head upon Mr. Leaver's shoulder, and Mr. Leaver grasping her hand with great fervour, and looking in her face from time to time with a melancholy and sympathetic aspect. The widow sat apart, feigning to be occupied with a book, but stealthily observing them from behind her fan; and the two firemen-watermen, smoking their pipes on the bank hard by, nudged each other, and grinned in enjoyment of the joke. Very few of the party missed the loving couple; and the few who did, heartily congratulated each other on their disappearance.

THE CONTRADICTORY COUPLE

One would suppose that two people who are to pass their whole lives together, and must necessarily be very often alone with each other, could find little pleasure in mutual contradiction; and yet what is more common than a contradictory couple?

The contradictory couple agree in nothing but contradiction. They return home from Mrs. Bluebottle's dinner-party, each in an opposite corner of the coach, and do not exchange a syllable until they have been seated for at least twenty minutes by the fireside at home, when the gentleman, raising his eyes from the stove, all at once breaks silence:

'What a very extraordinary thing it is,' says he, 'that you WILL contradict, Charlotte!' '_I_ contradict!' cries the lady, 'but that's just like you.' 'What's like me?' says the gentleman sharply. 'Saying that I contradict you,' replies the lady. 'Do you mean to say that you do NOT contradict me?' retorts the gentleman; 'do you mean to say that you have not been contradicting me the whole of this day?' 'Do you mean to tell me now, that you have not? I mean to tell you nothing of the kind,' replies the lady quietly; 'when you are wrong, of course I shall contradict you.'

During this dialogue the gentleman has been taking his brandy-and- water on one side of the fire, and the lady, with her dressing-case on the table, has been curling her hair on the other. She now lets down her back hair, and proceeds to brush it; preserving at the same time an air of conscious rectitude and suffering virtue, which is intended to exasperate the gentleman--and does so.

'I do believe,' he says, taking the spoon out of his glass, and tossing it on the table, 'that of all the obstinate, positive, wrong-headed creatures that were ever born, you are the most so, Charlotte.' 'Certainly, certainly, have it your own way, pray. You see how much _I_ contradict you,' rejoins the lady. 'Of course, you didn't contradict me at dinner-time--oh no, not you!' says the gentleman. 'Yes, I did,' says the lady. 'Oh, you did,' cries the gentleman 'you admit that?' 'If you call that contradiction, I do,' the lady answers; 'and I say again, Edward, that when I know you are wrong, I will contradict you. I am not your slave.' 'Not my slave!' repeats the gentleman bitterly; 'and you still mean to say that in the Blackburns' new house there are not more than fourteen doors, including the door of the wine- cellar!' 'I mean to say,' retorts the lady, beating time with her hair-brush on the palm of her hand, 'that in that house there are fourteen doors and no more.' 'Well then--' cries the gentleman, rising in despair, and pacing the room with rapid strides. 'By G-, this is enough to destroy a man's intellect, and drive him mad!'

By and by the gentleman comes-to a little, and passing his hand gloomily across his forehead, reseats himself in his former chair. There is a long silence, and this time the lady begins. 'I appealed to Mr. Jenkins, who sat next to me on the sofa in the drawing-room during tea--' 'Morgan, you mean,' interrupts the gentleman. 'I do not mean anything of the kind,' answers the lady. 'Now, by all that is aggravating and impossible to bear,' cries the gentleman, clenching his hands and looking up-wards in agony, 'she is going to insist upon it that Morgan is Jenkins!' 'Do you take me for a perfect fool?' exclaims the lady; 'do you suppose I don't know the one from the other? Do you suppose I don't know that the man in the blue coat was Mr. Jen-kins?' 'Jenkins in a blue coat!' cries the gentleman with a groan; 'Jenkins in a blue coat! a man who would suffer death rather than wear anything but brown!' 'Do you dare to charge me with telling an untruth?' demands the lady, bursting into tears. 'I charge you, ma'am,' retorts the gentleman, starting up, 'with being a monster of contradiction, a monster of aggravation, a--a--a--Jenkins in a blue coat!--what have I done that I should be doomed to hear such statements!'

Expressing himself with great scorn and anguish, the gentleman takes up his candle and stalks off to bed, where feigning to be fast asleep when the lady comes up-stairs drowned in tears, murmuring lamentations over her hard fate and in-distinct intentions of consulting her brothers, he undergoes the secret torture of hearing her exclaim between whiles, 'I know there are only fourteen doors in the house, I know it was Mr. Jenkins, I know he had a blue coat on, and I would say it as positively as I do now, if they were the last words I had to speak!'

If the contradictory couple are blessed with children, they are not the less con-tradictory on that account. Master James and Miss Charlotte present themselves af-ter dinner, and being in perfect good humour, and finding their parents in the same amiable state, augur from these appearances half a glass of wine a-piece and other extraordinary indulgences. But unfortunately Master James, growing talkative upon such prospects, asks his mamma how tall Mrs. Parsons is, and whether she is not six feet high; to which his mamma replies, 'Yes, she should think she was, for Mrs. Parsons is a very tall lady indeed; quite a giantess.' 'For Heaven's sake, Charlotte,' cries her husband, 'do not tell the child such preposterous nonsense. Six feet high!' 'Well,' replies the lady, 'surely I may be permitted to have an opinion; my opinion is, that she is six feet high--at least six feet.' 'Now you know, Charlotte,' retorts the gentleman sternly, 'that that is NOT your opinion--that you have no such idea--and that you only say this for the sake of contradiction.' 'You are exceedingly polite,' his wife replies; 'to be wrong about such a paltry question as anybody's height, would be no great crime; but I say again, that I believe Mrs. Parsons to be six feet-- more than six feet; nay, I believe you know her to be full six feet, and only say she is not, because I say she is.' This taunt disposes the gentleman to become violent, but he cheeks himself, and is content to mutter, in a haughty tone, 'Six feet--ha! ha! Mrs. Parsons six feet!' and the lady answers, 'Yes, six feet. I am sure I am glad you are amused, and I'll say it again--six feet.' Thus the subject gradually drops off, and the contradiction begins to be forgotten, when Master James, with some undefined notion of making himself agreeable, and putting things to rights again, unfortu- nately asks his mamma what the moon's made of; which gives her occasion to say that he had better not ask her, for she is always wrong and never can be right; that he only exposes her to contradiction by asking any question of her; and that he had better ask his papa, who is infallible, and never can be wrong. Papa, smarting under this attack, gives a terrible pull at the bell, and says, that if the conversation is to proceed in this way, the children had better be removed. Removed they are, after a few tears and many struggles; and Pa having looked at Ma sideways for a minute or two, with a baleful eye, draws his pocket-handkerchief over his face, and composes himself for his after-dinner nap.

The friends of the contradictory couple often deplore their frequent disputes, though they rather make light of them at the same time: observing, that there is no doubt they are very much attached to each other, and that they never quarrel except about trifles. But neither the friends of the contradictory couple, nor the contradictory couple themselves, reflect, that as the most stupendous objects in na- ture are but vast collections of minute particles, so the slightest and least considered trifles make up the sum of human happiness or misery.

THE COUPLE WHO DOTE
UPON THEIR CHILDREN

The couple who dote upon their children have usually a great many of them: six or eight at least. The children are either the healthiest in all the world, or the most unfortunate in existence. In either case, they are equally the theme of their doting parents, and equally a source of mental anguish and irritation to their doting parents' friends.

The couple who dote upon their children recognise no dates but those connected with their births, accidents, illnesses, or remarkable deeds. They keep a mental almanack with a vast number of Innocents'-days, all in red letters. They recollect the last coronation, because on that day little Tom fell down the kitchen stairs; the anniversary of the Gunpowder Plot, because it was on the fifth of November that Ned asked whether wooden legs were made in heaven and cocked hats grew in gardens. Mrs. Whiffler will never cease to recollect the last day of the old year as long as she lives, for it was on that day that the baby had the four red spots on its nose which they took for measles: nor Christmas-day, for twenty-one days after Christmas-day the twins were born; nor Good Friday, for it was on a Good Friday that she was frightened by the donkey-cart when she was in the family way with Georgiana. The movable feasts have no motion for Mr. and Mrs. Whiffler, but remain pinned down tight and fast to the shoulders of some small child, from whom they can never be separated any more. Time was made, according to their creed, not for slaves but for girls and boys; the restless sands in his glass are but little children at play.

As we have already intimated, the children of this couple can know no medium. They are either prodigies of good health or prodigies of bad health; whatever they are, they must be prodigies. Mr. Whiffler must have to describe at his office such excruciating agonies constantly undergone by his eldest boy, as nobody else's eldest boy ever underwent; or he must be able to declare that there never was a child endowed with such amazing health, such an indomitable constitution, and such a cast-iron frame, as his child. His children must be, in some respect or other, above and beyond the children of all other people. To such an extent is this feeling pushed, that we were once slightly acquainted with a lady and gentleman who carried their heads so high and became so proud after their youngest child fell out of a two-pair-of-stairs window without hurting himself much, that the greater part of their friends were obliged to forego their acquaintance. But perhaps this may be an extreme case, and one not justly entitled to be considered as a precedent of general application.

If a friend happen to dine in a friendly way with one of these couples who dote upon their children, it is nearly impossible for him to divert the conversation from their favourite topic. Everything reminds Mr. Whiffler of Ned, or Mrs. Whiffler of Mary Anne, or of the time before Ned was born, or the time before Mary Anne was thought of. The slightest remark, however harmless in itself, will awaken slumbering recollections of the twins. It is impossible to steer clear of them. They will come uppermost, let the poor man do what he may. Ned has been known to be lost sight of for half an hour, Dick has been forgotten, the name of Mary Anne has not been mentioned, but the twins will out. Nothing can keep down the twins.

'It's a very extraordinary thing, Saunders,' says Mr. Whiffler to the visitor, 'but--you have seen our little babies, the--the-- twins?' The friend's heart sinks within him as he answers, 'Oh, yes--often.' 'Your talking of the Pyramids,' says Mr. Whiffler, quite as a matter of course, 'reminds me of the twins. It's a very extraordinary thing about those babies--what colour should you say their eyes were?' 'Upon my word,' the friend stammers, 'I hardly know how to answer'--the fact being, that except as the friend does not remember to have heard of any departure from the ordinary course of nature in the instance of these twins, they might have no eyes at all for aught he has observed to the contrary. 'You wouldn't say they were red, I suppose?' says Mr. Whiffler. The friend hesitates, and rather thinks they are; but inferring from the expression of Mr. Whiffler's face that red is not the colour, smiles with some confidence, and says, 'No, no! very different from that.' 'What should you say to blue?' says Mr. Whiffler. The friend glances at him, and observing a different expression in his face, ventures to say, 'I should say they WERE blue--a decided blue.' 'To be sure!' cries Mr. Whiffler, triumphantly, 'I knew you would! But what should you say if I was to tell you that the boy's eyes are blue and the girl's hazel, eh?' 'Impossible!' exclaims the friend, not at all knowing why it should be impossible. 'A fact, notwithstanding,' cries Mr. Whiffler; 'and let me tell you, Saunders, THAT'S not a common thing in twins, or a circumstance that'll happen every day.'

In this dialogue Mrs. Whiffler, as being deeply responsible for the twins, their charms and singularities, has taken no share; but she now relates, in broken English, a witticism of little Dick's bearing upon the subject just discussed, which delights Mr. Whiffler beyond measure, and causes him to declare that he would have sworn that was Dick's if he had heard it anywhere. Then he requests that Mrs. Whiffler will tell Saunders what Tom said about mad bulls; and Mrs. Whiffler relating the anecdote, a discussion ensues upon the different character of Tom's wit and Dick's wit, from which it appears that Dick's humour is of a lively turn, while Tom's style is the dry and caustic. This discussion being enlivened by various illustrations, lasts a long time, and is only stopped by Mrs. Whiffler instructing the footman to ring the nursery bell, as the children were promised that they should come down and taste the pudding.

The friend turns pale when this order is given, and paler still when it is followed up by a great pattering on the staircase, (not unlike the sound of rain upon a skylight,) a violent bursting open of the dining-room door, and the tumultuous appearance of six small children, closely succeeded by a strong nursery-maid with a twin in each arm. As the whole eight are screaming, shouting, or kicking-- some influenced by a ravenous appetite, some by a horror of the stranger, and some by a conflict of the two feelings--a pretty long space elapses before all their heads can be ranged round the table and anything like order restored; in bringing about which happy state of things both the nurse and footman are severely scratched. At length Mrs. Whiffler is heard to say, 'Mr. Saunders, shall I give you some pudding?' A breathless silence ensues, and sixteen small eyes are fixed upon the guest in expectation of his reply. A wild shout of joy proclaims that he has said 'No, thank you.' Spoons are waved in the air, legs appear above the table-cloth in uncontrollable ecstasy, and eighty short fingers dabble in damson syrup.

While the pudding is being disposed of, Mr. and Mrs. Whiffler look on with beaming countenances, and Mr. Whiffler nudging his friend Saunders, begs him to take notice of Tom's eyes, or Dick's chin, or Ned's nose, or Mary Anne's hair, or

Emily's figure, or little Bob's calves, or Fanny's mouth, or Carry's head, as the case may be. Whatever the attention of Mr. Saunders is called to, Mr. Saunders admires of course; though he is rather confused about the sex of the youngest branches and looks at the wrong children, turning to a girl when Mr. Whiffler directs his attention to a boy, and falling into raptures with a boy when he ought to be enchanted with a girl. Then the dessert comes, and there is a vast deal of scrambling after fruit, and sudden spirting forth of juice out of tight oranges into infant eyes, and much screeching and wailing in consequence. At length it becomes time for Mrs. Whiffler to retire, and all the children are by force of arms compelled to kiss and love Mr. Saunders before going up-stairs, except Tom, who, lying on his back in the hall, proclaims that Mr. Saunders 'is a naughty beast;' and Dick, who having drunk his father's wine when he was looking another way, is found to be intoxicated and is carried out, very limp and helpless.

Mr. Whiffler and his friend are left alone together, but Mr. Whiffler's thoughts are still with his family, if his family are not with him. 'Saunders,' says he, after a short silence, 'if you please, we'll drink Mrs. Whiffler and the children.' Mr. Saunders feels this to be a reproach against himself for not proposing the same sentiment, and drinks it in some confusion. 'Ah!' Mr. Whiffler sighs, 'these children, Saunders, make one quite an old man.' Mr. Saunders thinks that if they were his, they would make him a very old man; but he says nothing. 'And yet,' pursues Mr. Whiffler, 'what can equal domestic happiness? what can equal the engaging ways of children! Saunders, why don't you get married?' Now, this is an embarrassing question, because Mr. Saunders has been thinking that if he had at any time entertained matrimonial designs, the revelation of that day would surely have routed them for ever. 'I am glad, however,' says Mr. Whiffler, 'that you ARE a bachelor,--glad on one account, Saunders; a selfish one, I admit. Will you do Mrs. Whiffler and myself a favour?' Mr. Saunders is surprised--evidently surprised; but he replies, 'with the greatest pleasure.' 'Then, will you, Saunders,' says Mr. Whiffler, in an impressive manner, 'will you cement and consolidate our friendship by coming into the family (so to speak) as a godfather?' 'I shall be proud and delighted,' replies Mr. Saunders: 'which of the children is it? really, I thought they were all christened; or--' 'Saunders,' Mr. Whiffler interposes, 'they ARE all christened; you are right. The fact is, that Mrs. Whiffler is--in short, we expect another.' 'Not a ninth!' cries the friend, all aghast at the idea. 'Yes, Saunders,' rejoins Mr. Whiffler, solemnly, 'a ninth. Did we drink Mrs. Whiffler's health? Let us drink it again, Saunders, and wish her well over it!'

Doctor Johnson used to tell a story of a man who had but one idea, which was a wrong one. The couple who dote upon their children are in the same predicament: at home or abroad, at all times, and in all places, their thoughts are bound up in this one subject, and have no sphere beyond. They relate the clever things their offspring say or do, and weary every company with their prolixity and absurdity. Mr. Whiffler takes a friend by the button at a street corner on a windy day to tell him a bon mot of his youngest boy's; and Mrs. Whiffler, calling to see a sick acquaintance, entertains her with a cheerful account of all her own past sufferings and present expectations. In such cases the sins of the fathers indeed descend upon the children; for people soon come to regard them as predestined little bores. The couple who dote upon their children cannot be said to be actuated by a general love for these engaging little people (which would be a great excuse); for they are apt to underrate and entertain a jealousy of any children but their own. If they examined their own hearts, they would, perhaps, find at the bottom of all this, more self-love and egotism than they think of. Self-love and egotism are bad qualities, of which the unrestrained exhibition, though it may be sometimes amusing, never fails to be wearisome and unpleasant. Couples who dote upon their children, therefore, are best avoided.

THE COOL COUPLE

There is an old-fashioned weather-glass representing a house with two doorways, in one of which is the figure of a gentleman, in the other the figure of a lady. When the weather is to be fine the lady comes out and the gentleman goes in; when wet, the gentleman comes out and the lady goes in. They never seek each other's society, are never elevated and depressed by the same cause, and have nothing in common. They are the model of a cool couple, except that there is something of politeness and consideration about the behaviour of the gentleman in the weather-glass, in which, neither of the cool couple can be said to participate.

The cool couple are seldom alone together, and when they are, nothing can exceed their apathy and dulness: the gentleman being for the most part drowsy, and the lady silent. If they enter into conversation, it is usually of an ironical or recriminatory nature. Thus, when the gentleman has indulged in a very long yawn and settled himself more snugly in his easy-chair, the lady will perhaps remark, 'Well, I am sure, Charles! I hope you're comfortable.' To which the gentleman replies, 'Oh yes, he's quite comfortable quite.' 'There are not many married men, I hope,' returns the lady, 'who seek comfort in such selfish gratifications as you do.' 'Nor many wives who seek comfort in such selfish gratifications as YOU do, I hope,' retorts the gentleman. 'Whose fault is that?' demands the lady. The gentleman becoming more sleepy, returns no answer. 'Whose fault is that?' the lady repeats. The gentleman still returning no answer, she goes on to say that she believes there never was in all this world anybody so attached to her home, so thoroughly domestic, so unwilling to seek a moment's gratification or pleasure beyond her own fireside as she. God knows that before she was married she never thought or dreamt of such a thing; and she remembers that her poor papa used to say again and again, almost every day of his life, 'Oh, my dear Louisa, if you only marry a man who understands you, and takes the trouble to consider your happiness and accommodate himself a very little to your disposition, what a treasure he will find in you!' She supposes her papa knew what her disposition was--he had known her long enough--he ought to have been acquainted with it, but what can she do? If her home is always dull and lonely, and her husband is always absent and finds no pleasure in her society, she is naturally sometimes driven (seldom enough, she is sure) to seek a little recreation elsewhere; she is not expected to pine and mope to death, she hopes. 'Then come, Louisa,' says the gentleman, waking up as suddenly as he fell asleep, 'stop at home this evening, and so will I.' 'I should be sorry to suppose, Charles, that you took a pleasure in aggravating me,' replies the lady; 'but you know as well as I do that I am particularly engaged to Mrs. Mortimer, and that it would be an act of the grossest rudeness and ill-breeding, after accepting a seat in her box and preventing her from inviting anybody else, not to go.' 'Ah! there it is!' says the gentleman, shrugging his shoulders, 'I knew that perfectly well. I knew you couldn't devote an evening to your own home. Now all I have to say, Louisa, is this--recollect that _I_ was quite willing to stay at home, and that it's no fault of MINE we are not oftener together.'

With that the gentleman goes away to keep an old appointment at his club, and the lady hurries off to dress for Mrs. Mortimer's; and neither thinks of the other until by some odd chance they find themselves alone again.

But it must not be supposed that the cool couple are habitually a quarrelsome one. Quite the contrary. These differences are only occasions for a little self-excuse,--nothing more. In general they are as easy and careless, and dispute as seldom, as any common acquaintances may; for it is neither worth their while to put each other out of the way, nor to ruffle themselves.

When they meet in society, the cool couple are the best-bred people in existence. The lady is seated in a corner among a little knot of lady friends, one of whom exclaims, 'Why, I vow and declare there is your husband, my dear!' 'Whose?--mine?' she says, carelessly. 'Ay, yours, and coming this way too.' 'How very odd!' says the lady, in a languid tone, 'I thought he had been at Dover.' The gentleman coming up, and speaking to all the other ladies and nodding slightly to his wife, it turns out that he has been at Dover, and has just now returned. 'What a strange creature you are!' cries his wife; 'and what on earth brought you here, I wonder?' 'I came to look after you, OF COURSE,' rejoins her husband. This is so pleasant a jest that the lady is mightily amused, as are all the other ladies similarly situated who are within hearing; and while they are enjoying it to the full, the gentleman nods again, turns upon his heel, and saunters away.

There are times, however, when his company is not so agreeable, though equally unexpected; such as when the lady has invited one or two particular friends to tea and scandal, and he happens to come home in the very midst of their diversion. It is a hundred chances to one that he remains in the house half an hour, but the lady is rather disturbed by the intrusion, notwithstanding, and reasons within herself,--'I am sure I never interfere with him, and why should he interfere with me? It can scarcely be accidental; it never happens that I have a particular reason for not wishing him to come home, but he always comes. It's very provoking and tiresome; and I am sure when he leaves me so much alone for his own pleasure, the least he could do would be to do as much for mine.' Observing what passes in her mind, the gentleman, who has come home for his own accommodation, makes a merit of it with himself; arrives at the conclusion that it is the very last place in which he can hope to be comfortable; and determines, as he takes up his hat and cane, never to be so virtuous again.

Thus a great many cool couples go on until they are cold couples, and the grave has closed over their folly and indifference. Loss of name, station, character, life itself, has ensued from causes as slight as these, before now; and when gossips tell such tales, and aggravate their deformities, they elevate their hands and eyebrows, and call each other to witness what a cool couple Mr. and Mrs. So- and-so always were, even in the best of times.

THE PLAUSIBLE COUPLE

The plausible couple have many titles. They are 'a delightful couple,' an 'affectionate couple,' 'a most agreeable couple, 'a good-hearted couple,' and 'the best-natured couple in existence.' The truth is, that the plausible couple are people of the world; and either the way of pleasing the world has grown much easier than it was in the days of the old man and his ass, or the old man was but a bad hand at it, and knew very little of the trade.

'But is it really possible to please the world!' says some doubting reader. It is indeed. Nay, it is not only very possible, but very easy. The ways are crooked, and sometimes foul and low. What then? A man need but crawl upon his hands and knees, know when to close his eyes and when his ears, when to stoop and when to stand upright; and if by the world is meant that atom of it in which he moves himself, he shall please it, never fear.

Now, it will be readily seen, that if a plausible man or woman have an easy means of pleasing the world by an adaptation of self to all its twistings and twinings, a plausible man AND woman, or, in other words, a plausible couple, playing into each other's hands, and acting in concert, have a manifest advantage. Hence it is that plausible couples scarcely ever fail of success on a pretty large scale; and hence it is that if the reader, laying down this unwieldy volume at the next full stop, will have the goodness to review his or her circle of acquaintance, and to search particularly for some man and wife with a large connexion and a good name, not easily referable to their abilities or their wealth, he or she (that is, the male or female reader) will certainly find that gentleman or lady, on a very short reflection, to be a plausible couple.

The plausible couple are the most ecstatic people living: the most sensitive people--to merit--on the face of the earth. Nothing clever or virtuous escapes them. They have microscopic eyes for such endowments, and can find them anywhere. The plausible couple never fawn--oh no! They don't even scruple to tell their friends of their faults. One is too generous, another too candid; a third has a tendency to think all people like himself, and to regard mankind as a company of angels; a fourth is kind-hearted to a fault. 'We never flatter, my dear Mrs. Jackson,' say the plausible couple; 'we speak our minds. Neither you nor Mr. Jackson have faults enough. It may sound strangely, but it is true. You have not faults enough. You know our way,--we must speak out, and always do. Quarrel with us for saying so, if you will; but we repeat it,--you have not faults enough!'

The plausible couple are no less plausible to each other than to third parties. They are always loving and harmonious. The plausible gentleman calls his wife 'darling,' and the plausible lady addresses him as 'dearest.' If it be Mr. and Mrs. Bobtail Widger, Mrs. Widger is 'Lavinia, darling,' and Mr. Widger is 'Bobtail, dearest.' Speaking of each other, they observe the same tender form. Mrs. Widger relates what 'Bobtail' said, and Mr. Widger recounts what 'darling' thought and did.

If you sit next to the plausible lady at a dinner-table, she takes the earliest opportunity of expressing her belief that you are acquainted with the Clickits; she is sure she has heard the Clickits speak of you--she must not tell you in what terms, or you will take her for a flatterer. You admit a knowledge of the Clickits; the plausible lady immediately launches out in their praise. She quite loves the Clickits. Were there ever such true- hearted, hospitable, excellent people--such a gentle, interesting little woman as Mrs. Clickit, or such a frank, unaffected creature as Mr. Clickit? were there ever two people, in short, so little spoiled by the world as they are? 'As who, darling?' cries Mr. Widger, from the opposite side of the table. 'The Clickits, dearest,' replies Mrs. Widger. 'Indeed you are right, darling,' Mr. Widger rejoins; 'the Clickits are a very high-minded, worthy, estimable couple.' Mrs. Widger remarking that Bobtail always grows quite eloquent upon this subject, Mr. Widger admits that he feels very strongly whenever such people as the Clickits and some other friends of his (here he glances at the host and hostess) are mentioned;

for they are an honour to human nature, and do one good to think of. 'YOU know the Clickits, Mrs. Jackson?' he says, addressing the lady of the house. 'No, indeed; we have not that pleasure,' she replies. 'You astonish me!' exclaims Mr. Widger: 'not know the Clickits! why, you are the very people of all others who ought to be their bosom friends. You are kindred beings; you are one and the same thing:- not know the Clickits! Now WILL you know the Clickits? Will you make a point of knowing them? Will you meet them in a friendly way at our house one evening, and be acquainted with them?' Mrs. Jackson will be quite delighted; nothing would give her more pleasure. 'Then, Lavinia, my darling,' says Mr. Widger, 'mind you don't lose sight of that; now, pray take care that Mr. and Mrs. Jackson know the Clickits without loss of time. Such people ought not to be strangers to each other.' Mrs. Widger books both families as the centre of attraction for her next party; and Mr. Widger, going on to expatiate upon the virtues of the Clickits, adds to their other moral qualities, that they keep one of the neatest phaetons in town, and have two thousand a year.

As the plausible couple never laud the merits of any absent person, without dexterously contriving that their praises shall reflect upon somebody who is present, so they never depreciate anything or anybody, without turning their depreciation to the same account. Their friend, Mr. Slummery, say they, is unquestionably a clever painter, and would no doubt be very popular, and sell his pictures at a very high price, if that cruel Mr. Fithers had not forestalled him in his department of art, and made it thoroughly and completely his own;--Fithers, it is to be observed, being present and within hearing, and Slummery elsewhere. Is Mrs. Tabblewick really as beautiful as people say? Why, there indeed you ask them a very puzzling question, because there is no doubt that she is a very charming woman, and they have long known her intimately. She is no doubt beautiful, very beautiful; they once thought her the most beautiful woman ever seen; still if you press them for an honest answer, they are bound to say that this was before they had ever seen our lovely friend on the sofa, (the sofa is hard by, and our lovely friend can't help hearing the whispers in which this is said;) since that time, perhaps, they have been hardly fair judges; Mrs. Tabblewick is no doubt extremely handsome,--very like our friend, in fact, in the form of the features,--but in point of expression, and soul, and figure, and air altogether--oh dear!

But while the plausible couple depreciate, they are still careful to preserve their character for amiability and kind feeling; indeed the depreciation itself is often made to grow out of their excessive sympathy and good will. The plausible lady calls on a lady who dotes upon her children, and is sitting with a little girl upon her knee, enraptured by her artless replies, and protesting that there is nothing she delights in so much as conversing with these fairies; when the other lady inquires if she has seen young Mrs. Finching lately, and whether the baby has turned out a finer one than it promised to be. 'Oh dear!' cries the plausible lady, 'you cannot think how often Bobtail and I have talked about poor Mrs. Finching--she is such a dear soul, and was so anxious that the baby should be a fine child--and very naturally, because she was very much here at one time, and there is, you know, a natural emulation among mothers--that it is impossible to tell you how much we have felt for her.' 'Is it weak or plain, or what?' inquires the other. 'Weak or plain, my love,' returns the plausible lady, 'it's a fright--a perfect little fright; you never saw such a miserable creature in all your days. Positively you must not let her see one of these beautiful dears again, or you'll break her heart, you will indeed.--Heaven bless this child, see how she is looking in my face! can you conceive anything prettier than that? If poor Mrs. Finching could only hope--but that's impossible--and the gifts of Providence, you know--What DID I do with my pocket- handkerchief!'

What prompts the mother, who dotes upon her children, to comment to her lord that evening on the plausible lady's engaging qualities and feeling heart, and what is it that procures Mr. and Mrs. Bobtail Widger an immediate invitation to dinner?

THE NICE LITTLE COUPLE

A custom once prevailed in old-fashioned circles, that when a lady or gentleman was unable to sing a song, he or she should enliven the company with a story. As we find ourself in the predicament of not being able to describe (to our own satisfaction) nice little couples in the abstract, we purpose telling in this place a little story about a nice little couple of our acquaintance.

Mr. and Mrs. Chirrup are the nice little couple in question. Mr. Chirrup has the smartness, and something of the brisk, quick manner of a small bird. Mrs. Chirrup is the prettiest of all little women, and has the prettiest little figure conceivable. She has the neatest little foot, and the softest little voice, and the pleasantest little smile, and the tidiest little curls, and the brightest little eyes, and the quietest little manner, and is, in short, altogether one of the most engaging of all little women, dead or alive. She is a condensation of all the domestic virtues,- -a pocket edition of the young man's best companion,--a little woman at a very high pressure, with an amazing quantity of goodness and usefulness in an exceedingly small space. Little as she is, Mrs. Chirrup might furnish forth matter for the moral equipment of a score of housewives, six feet high in their stockings--if, in the presence of ladies, we may be allowed the expression--and of corresponding robustness.

Nobody knows all this better than Mr. Chirrup, though he rather takes on that he don't. Accordingly he is very proud of his better-half, and evidently considers himself, as all other people consider him, rather fortunate in having her to wife. We say evidently, because Mr. Chirrup is a warm-hearted little fellow; and if you catch his eye when he has been slyly glancing at Mrs. Chirrup in company, there is a certain complacent twinkle in it, accompanied, perhaps, by a half-expressed toss of the head, which as clearly indicates what has been passing in his mind as if he had put it into words, and shouted it out through a speaking-trumpet. Moreover, Mr. Chirrup has a particularly mild and bird-like manner of calling Mrs. Chirrup 'my dear;' and--for he is of a jocose turn- -of cutting little witticisms upon her, and making her the subject of various harmless pleasantries, which nobody enjoys more thoroughly than Mrs. Chirrup herself. Mr. Chirrup, too, now and then affects to deplore his bachelor-days, and to bemoan (with a marvellously contented and smirking face) the loss of his freedom, and the sorrow of his heart at having been taken captive by Mrs. Chirrup--all of which circumstances combine to show the secret triumph and satisfaction of Mr. Chirrup's soul.

We have already had occasion to observe that Mrs. Chirrup is an incomparable housewife. In all the arts of domestic arrangement and management, in all the mysteries of confectionery-making, pickling, and preserving, never was such a thorough adept as that nice little body. She is, besides, a cunning worker in muslin and fine linen, and a special hand at marketing to the very best advantage. But if there be one branch of housekeeping in which she excels to an utterly unparalleled and unprecedented extent, it is in the important one of carving. A roast goose is universally allowed to be the great stumbling-block in the way of young aspirants to perfection in this department of science; many promising carvers, beginning with legs of mutton, and preserving a good reputation through fillets of veal, sirloins of beef, quarters of lamb, fowls, and even ducks, have sunk before a roast goose, and lost caste and character for ever. To Mrs. Chirrup the resolving a goose into its smallest component parts is a pleasant pastime--a practical joke--a thing to be done in a minute or so, without the smallest interruption to the conversation of the time. No handing the dish over to an unfortunate man upon her right or left, no wild sharpening of the knife, no hacking and sawing at an unruly joint, no noise, no splash, no heat, no leaving off in despair; all is confidence and cheerfulness. The dish is set upon the table, the cover is removed; for an instant, and only an instant, you observe that Mrs. Chirrup's attention is distracted; she smiles, but heareth not. You proceed with your story; meanwhile the glittering knife is slowly upraised, both Mrs. Chirrup's wrists are slightly but not ungracefully agitated, she compresses her lips for an instant, then breaks into a smile, and all is over. The legs of the bird slide gently down into a pool of gravy, the wings seem to melt from the body, the breast separates into a row of juicy slices, the smaller and more complicated parts of his anatomy are perfectly developed, a cavern of stuffing is revealed, and the goose is gone!

To dine with Mr. and Mrs. Chirrup is one of the pleasantest things in the world. Mr. Chirrup has a bachelor friend, who lived with him in his own days of single blessedness, and to whom he is mightily attached. Contrary to the usual custom, this bachelor friend is no less a friend of Mrs. Chirrup's, and, consequently, whenever you dine with Mr. and Mrs. Chirrup, you meet the bachelor friend. It would put any reasonably-conditioned mortal into good- humour to observe the entire unanimity which subsists between these three; but there is a quiet welcome dimpling in Mrs. Chirrup's face, a bustling hospitality oozing as it were out of the waistcoat-pockets of Mr. Chirrup, and a patronising enjoyment of their cordiality and satisfaction on the part of the bachelor friend, which is quite delightful. On these occasions Mr. Chirrup usually takes an opportunity of rallying the friend on being single, and the friend retorts on Mr. Chirrup for being married, at which moments some single young ladies present are like to die of laughter; and we have more than once observed them bestow looks upon the friend, which convinces us that his position is by no means a safe one, as, indeed, we hold no bachelor's to be who visits married friends and cracks jokes on wedlock, for certain it is that such men walk among traps and nets and pitfalls innumerable, and often find themselves down upon their knees at the altar rails, taking M. or N. for their wedded wives, before they know anything about the matter.

However, this is no business of Mr. Chirrup's, who talks, and laughs, and drinks his wine, and laughs again, and talks more, until it is time to repair to the drawing-room, where, coffee served and over, Mrs. Chirrup prepares for a round game, by sorting the nicest possible little fish into the nicest possible little pools, and calling Mr. Chirrup to assist her, which Mr. Chirrup does. As they stand side by side, you find that Mr. Chirrup is the least possible shadow of a shade taller than Mrs. Chirrup, and that they are the neatest and best-matched little couple that can be, which the chances are ten to one against your observing with such effect at any other time, unless you see them in the street arm-in- arm, or meet them some rainy day trotting along under a very small umbrella. The round game (at which Mr. Chirrup is the merriest of the party) being done and over, in course of time a nice little tray appears, on which is a nice little supper; and when that is finished likewise, and you have said 'Good night,' you find yourself repeating a dozen times, as you ride home, that there never was such a nice little couple as Mr. and Mrs. Chirrup.

Whether it is that pleasant qualities, being packed more closely in small bodies than in large, come more readily to hand than when they are diffused over a wider space, and have to be gathered together for use, we don't know, but as a general rule,-- strengthened like all other rules by its exceptions,--we hold that little people are sprightly and good-natured. The more sprightly and good-natured people we have, the better; therefore, let us wish well to all nice little couples, and hope that they may increase and multiply.

THE EGOTISTICAL COUPLE

Egotism in couples is of two kinds.--It is our purpose to show this by two examples.

The egotistical couple may be young, old, middle-aged, well to do, or ill to do; they may have a small family, a large family, or no family at all. There is no outward sign by which an egotistical couple may be known and avoided. They come upon you unawares; there is no guarding against them. No man can of himself be forewarned or forearmed against an egotistical couple.

The egotistical couple have undergone every calamity, and experienced every pleasurable and painful sensation of which our nature is susceptible. You cannot by possibility tell the egotistical couple anything they don't know, or describe to them anything they have not felt. They have been everything but dead. Sometimes we are tempted to wish they had been even that, but only in our uncharitable moments, which are few and far between.

We happened the other day, in the course of a morning call, to encounter an egotistical couple, nor were we suffered to remain long in ignorance of the fact, for our very first inquiry of the lady of the house brought them into active and vigorous operation. The inquiry was of course touching the lady's health, and the answer happened to be, that she had not been very well. 'Oh, my dear!' said the egotistical lady, 'don't talk of not being well. We have been in SUCH a state since we saw you last!'--The lady of the house happening to remark that her lord had not been well either, the egotistical gentleman struck in: 'Never let Briggs complain of not being well--never let Briggs complain, my dear Mrs. Briggs, after what I have undergone within these six weeks. He doesn't know what it is to be ill, he hasn't the least idea of it; not the faintest conception.'--'My dear,' interposed his wife smiling, 'you talk as if it were almost a crime in Mr. Briggs not to have been as ill as we have been, instead of feeling thankful to Providence that both he and our dear Mrs. Briggs are in such blissful ignorance of real suffering.'--'My love,' returned the egotistical gentleman, in a low and pious voice, 'you mistake me;-- I feel grateful--very grateful. I trust our friends may never purchase their experience as dearly as we have bought ours; I hope they never may!'

Having put down Mrs. Briggs upon this theme, and settled the question thus, the egotistical gentleman turned to us, and, after a few preliminary remarks, all tending towards and leading up to the point he had in his mind, inquired if we happened to be acquainted with the Dowager Lady Snorflerer. On our replying in the negative, he presumed we had often met Lord Slang, or beyond all doubt, that we were on intimate terms with Sir Chipkins Glogwog. Finding that we were equally unable to lay claim to either of these distinctions, he expressed great astonishment, and turning to his wife with a retrospective smile, inquired who it was that had told that capital story about the mashed potatoes. 'Who, my dear?' returned the egotistical lady, 'why Sir Chipkins, of course; how can you ask! Don't you remember his applying it to our cook, and saying that you and I were so like the Prince and Princess, that he could almost have sworn we were they?' 'To be sure, I remember that,' said the egotistical gentleman, 'but are you quite certain that didn't apply to the other anecdote about the Emperor of Austria and the pump?' 'Upon my word then, I think it did,' replied his wife. 'To be sure it did,' said the egotistical gentleman, 'it was Slang's story, I remember now, perfectly.' However, it turned out, a few seconds afterwards, that the egotistical gentleman's memory was rather treacherous, as he began to have a misgiving that the story had been told by the Dowager Lady Snorflerer the very last time they dined there; but there appearing, on further consideration, strong circumstantial evidence tending to show that this couldn't be, inasmuch as the Dowager Lady Snorflerer had been, on the occasion in question, wholly engrossed by the egotistical lady, the egotistical gentleman recanted this opinion; and after laying the story at the doors of a great many great people, happily left it at last with the Duke of Scuttlewig:- observing that it was not extraordinary he had forgotten his Grace hitherto, as it often happened that the names of those with whom we were upon the most familiar footing were the very last to present themselves to our thoughts.

It not only appeared that the egotistical couple knew everybody, but that scarcely any event of importance or notoriety had occurred for many years with which they had not been in some way or other connected. Thus we learned that when the well-known attempt upon the life of George the Third was made by Hatfield in Drury Lane theatre, the egotistical gentleman's grandfather sat upon his right hand and was the first man who collared him; and that the egotistical lady's aunt, sitting within a few boxes of the royal party, was the only person in the audience who heard his Majesty exclaim, 'Charlotte, Charlotte, don't be frightened, don't be frightened; they're letting off squibs, they're letting off squibs.' When the fire broke out, which ended in the destruction of the two Houses of Parliament, the egotistical couple, being at the time at a drawing-room window on Blackheath, then and there simultaneously exclaimed, to the astonishment of a whole party-- 'It's the House of Lords!' Nor was this a solitary instance of their peculiar discernment, for chancing to be (as by a comparison of dates and circumstances they afterwards found) in the same omnibus with Mr. Greenacre, when he carried his victim's head about town in a blue bag, they both remarked a singular twitching in the muscles of his countenance; and walking down Fish Street Hill, a few weeks since, the egotistical gentleman said to his lady-- slightly casting up his eyes to the top of the Monument--'There's a boy up there, my dear, reading a Bible. It's very strange. I don't like it.--In five seconds afterwards, Sir,' says the egotistical gentleman, bringing his hands together with one violent clap--'the lad was over!'

Diversifying these topics by the introduction of many others of the same kind, and entertaining us between whiles with a minute account of what weather and diet agreed with them, and what weather and diet disagreed with them, and at what time they usually got up, and at what time went to bed, with many other particulars of their domestic economy too numerous to mention; the egotistical couple at length took their leave, and afforded us an opportunity of doing the same.

Mr. and Mrs. Sliverstone are an egotistical couple of another class, for all the lady's egotism is about her husband, and all the gentleman's about his wife. For example:- Mr. Sliverstone is a clerical gentleman, and occasionally writes sermons, as clerical gentlemen do. If you happen to obtain admission at the street-door while he is so engaged, Mrs. Sliverstone appears on tip-toe, and speaking in a solemn whisper, as if there were at least three or four particular friends up-stairs, all upon the point of death, implores you to be very silent, for Mr. Sliverstone is composing, and she need not say how very important it is that he should not be disturbed. Unwilling to interrupt anything so serious, you hasten to withdraw, with many apologies; but this Mrs. Sliverstone will by no means allow, observing, that she knows you would like to see him, as it is very natural you should, and that she is determined to make a trial for you, as you are a great favourite. So you are led up-stairs--still on tip-toe--to the door of a little back room, in which, as the lady informs you in a whisper, Mr. Sliverstone always writes. No answer being returned to a couple of soft taps, the lady opens the door, and there, sure enough, is Mr. Sliverstone, with dishevelled hair, powdering away with pen, ink, and paper, at a rate which, if he has any power of sustaining it, would settle the longest sermon in no time. At first he is too much absorbed to be roused by this intrusion; but presently looking up, says faintly, 'Ah!' and pointing to his desk with a weary and languid smile, extends his hand, and hopes you'll forgive him. Then Mrs. Sliverstone sits down beside him, and taking his hand in hers, tells you how that Mr. Sliverstone has been shut up there ever since nine o'clock in the morning, (it is by this time twelve at noon,) and how she knows it cannot be good for his health, and is very uneasy about it. Unto this Mr. Sliverstone replies firmly, that 'It must be done;' which agonizes Mrs. Sliverstone still more, and she goes on to tell you that such were Mr. Sliverstone's labours last week--what with the buryings, marryings, churchings, christenings, and all together,--that when he was going up the pulpit stairs on Sunday evening, he was obliged to hold on by the rails, or he would certainly have fallen over into his own pew. Mr. Sliverstone, who has been listening and smiling meekly, says, 'Not quite so bad as that, not quite so bad!' he admits though, on cross-examination, that he WAS very near falling upon the verger who was following him up to bolt the door; but adds, that it was his duty as a Christian to fall upon him, if need were, and that he, Mr. Sliverstone, and (possibly the verger too) ought to glory in it.

This sentiment communicates new impulse to Mrs. Sliverstone, who launches into new praises of Mr. Sliverstone's worth and excellence, to which he listens in the same meek silence, save when he puts in a word of self-denial relative to some question of fact, as--'Not seventy-two christenings that week, my dear. Only seventy-one, only seventy-one.' At length his lady has quite concluded, and then he says, Why should he repine, why should he give way, why should he suffer his heart to sink within him? Is it he alone who toils and suffers? What has she gone through, he should like to know? What does she go through every day for him and for society?

With such an exordium Mr. Sliverstone launches out into glowing praises of the conduct of Mrs. Sliverstone in the production of eight young children, and the subsequent rearing and fostering of the same; and thus the husband magnifies the wife, and the wife the husband.

This would be well enough if Mr. and Mrs. Sliverstone kept it to themselves, or even to themselves and a friend or two; but they do not. The more hearers they have, the more egotistical the couple become, and the more anxious they are to make believers in their merits. Perhaps this is the worst kind of egotism. It has not even the poor excuse of being spontaneous, but is the result of a deliberate system and malice aforethought. Mere empty-headed conceit excites our pity, but ostentatious hypocrisy awakens our disgust.

THE COUPLE WHO CODDLE THEMSELVES

Mrs. Merrywinkle's maiden name was Chopper. She was the only child of Mr. and Mrs. Chopper. Her father died when she was, as the play-books express it, 'yet an infant;' and so old Mrs. Chopper, when her daughter married, made the house of her son-in-law her home from that time henceforth, and set up her staff of rest with Mr. and Mrs. Merrywinkle.

Mr. and Mrs. Merrywinkle are a couple who coddle themselves; and the venerable Mrs. Chopper is an aider and abettor in the same.

Mr. Merrywinkle is a rather lean and long-necked gentleman, middle- aged and middle-sized, and usually troubled with a cold in the head. Mrs. Merrywinkle is a delicate-looking lady, with very light hair, and is exceedingly subject to the same unpleasant disorder. The venerable Mrs. Chopper--who is strictly entitled to the appellation, her daughter not being very young, otherwise than by courtesy, at the time of her marriage, which was some years ago--is a mysterious old lady who lurks behind a pair of spectacles, and is afflicted with a chronic disease, respecting which she has taken a vast deal of medical advice, and referred to a vast number of medical books, without meeting any definition of symptoms that at all suits her, or enables her to say, 'That's my complaint.' Indeed, the absence of authentic information upon the subject of this complaint would seem to be Mrs. Chopper's greatest ill, as in all other respects she is an uncommonly hale and hearty gentlewoman.

Both Mr. and Mrs. Chopper wear an extraordinary quantity of flannel, and have a habit of putting their feet in hot water to an unnatural extent. They likewise indulge in chamomile tea and such- like compounds, and rub themselves on the slightest provocation with camphorated spirits and other lotions applicable to mumps, sore-throat, rheumatism, or lumbago.

Mr. Merrywinkle's leaving home to go to business on a damp or wet morning is a very elaborate affair. He puts on wash-leather socks over his stockings, and India-rubber shoes above his boots, and wears under his waistcoat a cuirass of hare-skin. Besides these precautions, he winds a thick shawl round his throat, and blocks up his mouth with a large silk handkerchief. Thus accoutred, and furnished besides with a great-coat and umbrella, he braves the dangers of the streets; travelling in severe weather at a gentle trot, the better to preserve the circulation, and bringing his mouth to the surface to take breath, but very seldom, and with the utmost caution. His office-door opened, he shoots past his clerk at the same pace, and diving into his own private room, closes the door, examines the window-fastenings, and gradually unrobes himself: hanging his pocket-handkerchief on the fender to air, and determining to write to the newspapers about the fog, which, he says, 'has really got to that pitch that it is quite unbearable.'

In this last opinion Mrs. Merrywinkle and her respected mother fully concur; for though not present, their thoughts and tongues are occupied with the same subject, which is their constant theme all day. If anybody happens to call, Mrs. Merrywinkle opines that they must assuredly be mad, and her first salutation is, 'Why, what in the name of goodness can bring you out in such weather? You know you MUST catch your death.' This assurance is corroborated by Mrs. Chopper, who adds, in further confirmation, a dismal legend concerning an individual of her acquaintance who, making a call under precisely parallel circumstances, and being then in the best health and spirits, expired in forty-eight hours afterwards, of a complication of inflammatory disorders. The visitor, rendered not altogether comfortable perhaps by this and other precedents, inquires very affectionately after Mr. Merrywinkle, but by so doing brings about no change of the subject; for Mr. Merrywinkle's name is inseparably connected with his complaints, and his complaints are inseparably connected with Mrs. Merrywinkle's; and when these are done with, Mrs. Chopper, who has been biding her time, cuts in with the chronic disorder--a subject upon which the amiable old lady never leaves off speaking until she is left alone, and very often not then.

But Mr. Merrywinkle comes home to dinner. He is received by Mrs. Merrywinkle and Mrs. Chopper, who, on his remarking that he thinks his feet are damp, turn pale as ashes and drag him up-stairs, imploring him to have them rubbed directly with a dry coarse towel. Rubbed they are, one by Mrs. Merrywinkle and one by Mrs. Chopper, until the friction causes Mr. Merrywinkle to make horrible faces, and look as if he had been smelling very powerful onions; when they desist, and the patient, provided for his better security with thick worsted stockings and list slippers, is borne down-stairs to dinner. Now, the dinner is always a good one, the appetites of the diners being delicate, and requiring a little of what Mrs. Merrywinkle calls 'tittivation;' the secret of which is understood to lie in good cookery and tasteful spices, and which process is so successfully performed in the present instance, that both Mr. and Mrs. Merrywinkle eat a remarkably good dinner, and even the afflicted Mrs. Chopper wields her knife and fork with much of the spirit and elasticity of youth. But Mr. Merrywinkle, in his desire to gratify his appetite, is not unmindful of his health, for he has a bottle of carbonate of soda with which to qualify his porter, and a little pair of scales in which to weigh it out. Neither in his anxiety to take care of his body is he unmindful of the welfare of his immortal part, as he always prays that for what he is going to receive he may be made truly thankful; and in order that he may be as thankful as possible, eats and drinks to the utmost.

Either from eating and drinking so much, or from being the victim of this constitutional infirmity, among others, Mr. Merrywinkle, after two or three glasses of wine, falls fast asleep; and he has scarcely closed his eyes, when Mrs. Merrywinkle and Mrs. Chopper fall asleep likewise. It is on awakening at tea-time that their most alarming symptoms prevail; for then Mr. Merrywinkle feels as if his temples were tightly bound round with the chain of the street-door, and Mrs. Merrywinkle as if she had made a hearty dinner of half-hundredweights, and Mrs. Chopper as if cold water were running down her back, and oyster-knives with sharp points were plunging of their own accord into her ribs. Symptoms like these are enough to make people peevish, and no wonder that they remain so until supper-time, doing little more than doze and complain, unless Mr. Merrywinkle calls out very loudly to a servant 'to keep that draught out,' or rushes into the passage to flourish his fist in the countenance of the twopenny-postman, for daring to give such a knock as he had just performed at the door of a private gentleman with nerves.

Supper, coming after dinner, should consist of some gentle provocative; and therefore the tittivating art is again in requisition, and again--done honour to by Mr. and Mrs. Merrywinkle, still comforted and abetted by Mrs. Chopper. After supper, it is ten to one but the last-named old lady becomes worse, and is led off to bed with the chronic complaint in full vigour. Mr. and Mrs. Merrywinkle, having administered to her a warm cordial, which is something of the strongest, then repair to their own room, where Mr. Merrywinkle, with his legs and feet in hot water, superintends the mulling of some wine which he is to drink at the very moment he plunges into bed, while Mrs. Merrywinkle, in garments whose nature is unknown to and unimagined by all but married men, takes four small pills with a spasmodic look between each, and finally comes to something hot and fragrant out of another little saucepan, which serves as her composing-draught for the night.

There is another kind of couple who coddle themselves, and who do so at a cheaper rate and on more spare diet, because they are niggardly and parsimonious; for which reason they are kind enough to coddle their visitors too. It is unnecessary to describe them, for our readers may rest assured of the accuracy of these general principles:- that all couples who coddle themselves are selfish and slothful,--that they charge upon every wind that blows, every rain that falls, and every vapour that hangs in the air, the evils which arise from their own imprudence or the gloom which is engendered in their own tempers,--and that all men and women, in couples or otherwise, who fall into exclusive habits of self-indulgence, and forget their natural sympathy and close connexion with everybody and everything in the world around them, not only neglect the first duty of life, but, by a happy retributive justice, deprive themselves of its truest and best enjoyment.

THE OLD COUPLE

They are grandfather and grandmother to a dozen grown people and have great-grandchildren besides; their bodies are bent, their hair is grey, their step tottering and infirm. Is this the lightsome pair whose wedding was so merry, and have the young couple indeed grown old so soon!

It seems but yesterday--and yet what a host of cares and griefs are crowded into the intervening time which, reckoned by them, lengthens out into a century! How many new associations have wreathed themselves about their hearts since then! The old time is gone, and a new time has come for others--not for them. They are but the rusting link that feebly joins the two, and is silently loosening its hold and dropping asunder.

It seems but yesterday--and yet three of their children have sunk into the grave, and the tree that shades it has grown quite old. One was an infant--they wept for him; the next a girl, a slight young thing too delicate for earth--her loss was hard indeed to bear. The third, a man. That was the worst of all, but even that grief is softened now.

It seems but yesterday--and yet how the gay and laughing faces of that bright morning have changed and vanished from above ground! Faint likenesses of some remain about them yet, but they are very faint and scarcely to be traced. The rest are only seen in dreams, and even they are unlike what they were, in eyes so old and dim.

One or two dresses from the bridal wardrobe are yet preserved. They are of a quaint and antique fashion, and seldom seen except in pictures. White has turned yellow, and brighter hues have faded. Do you wonder, child? The wrinkled face was once as smooth as yours, the eyes as bright, the shrivelled skin as fair and delicate. It is the work of hands that have been dust these many years.

Where are the fairy lovers of that happy day whose annual return comes upon the old man and his wife, like the echo of some village bell which has long been silent? Let yonder peevish bachelor, racked by rheumatic pains, and quarrelling with the world, let him answer to the question. He recollects something of a favourite playmate; her name was Lucy--so they tell him. He is not sure whether she was married, or went abroad, or died. It is a long while ago, and he don't remember.

Is nothing as it used to be; does no one feel, or think, or act, as in days of yore? Yes. There is an aged woman who once lived servant with the old lady's father, and is sheltered in an alms- house not far off. She is still attached to the family, and loves them all; she nursed the children in her lap, and tended in their sickness those who are no more. Her old mistress has still something of youth in her eyes; the young ladies are like what she was but not quite so handsome, nor are the gentlemen as stately as Mr. Harvey used to be. She has seen a great deal of trouble; her husband and her son died long ago; but she has got over that, and is happy now-- quite happy.

If ever her attachment to her old protectors were disturbed by fresher cares and hopes, it has long since resumed its former current. It has filled the void in the poor creature's heart, and replaced the love of kindred. Death has not left her alone, and this, with a roof above her head, and a warm hearth to sit by, makes her cheerful and contented. Does she remember the marriage of great-grandmamma? Ay, that she does, as well--as if it was only yesterday. You wouldn't think it to look at her now, and perhaps she ought not to say so of herself, but she was as smart a young girl then as you'd wish to see. She recollects she took a friend of hers up-stairs to see Miss Emma dressed for church; her name was--ah! she forgets the name, but she remembers that she was a very pretty girl, and that she married not long afterwards, and lived--it has quite passed out of her mind where she lived, but she knows she had a bad husband who used her ill, and that she died in Lambeth work-house. Dear, dear, in Lambeth workhouse!

And the old couple--have they no comfort or enjoyment of existence? See them among their grandchildren and great-grandchildren; how garrulous they are, how they compare one with another, and insist on likenesses which no one else can see; how gently the old lady lectures the girls on points of breeding and decorum, and points the moral by anecdotes of herself in her young days--how the old gentleman chuckles over boyish feats and roguish tricks, and tells long stories of a 'barring-out' achieved at the school he went to: which was very wrong, he tells the boys, and never to be imitated of course, but which he cannot help letting them know was very pleasant too--especially when he kissed the master's niece. This last, however, is a point on which the old lady is very tender, for she considers it a shocking and indelicate thing to talk about, and always says so whenever it is mentioned, never failing to observe that he ought to be very penitent for having been so sinful. So the old gentleman gets no further, and what the schoolmaster's niece said afterwards (which he is always going to tell) is lost to posterity.

The old gentleman is eighty years old, to-day--'Eighty years old, Crofts, and never had a headache,' he tells the barber who shaves him (the barber being a young fellow, and very subject to that complaint). 'That's a great age, Crofts,' says the old gentleman. 'I don't think it's sich a wery great age, Sir,' replied the barber. 'Crofts,' rejoins the old gentleman, 'you're talking nonsense to me. Eighty not a great age?' 'It's a wery great age, Sir, for a gentleman to be as healthy and active as you are,' returns the barber; 'but my grandfather, Sir, he was ninety-four.' 'You don't mean that, Crofts?' says the old gentleman. 'I do indeed, Sir,' retorts the barber, 'and as wiggerous as Julius Caesar, my grandfather was.' The old gentleman muses a little time, and then says, 'What did he die of, Crofts?' 'He died accidentally, Sir,' returns the barber; 'he didn't mean to do it. He always would go a running about the streets--walking never satisfied HIS spirit--and he run against a post and died of a hurt in his chest.' The old gentleman says no more until the shaving is concluded, and then he gives Crofts half-a-crown to drink his health. He is a little doubtful of the barber's veracity afterwards, and telling the anecdote to the old lady, affects to make very light of it--though to be sure (he adds) there was old Parr, and in some parts of England, ninety-five or so is a common age, quite a common age.

This morning the old couple are cheerful but serious, recalling old times as well as they can remember them, and dwelling upon many passages in their past lives which the day brings to mind. The old lady reads aloud, in a tremulous voice, out of a great Bible, and the old gentleman with his hand to his ear, listens with profound respect. When the book is closed, they sit silent for a short space, and afterwards resume their conversation, with a reference perhaps to their dead children, as a subject not unsuited to that they have just left. By degrees they are led to consider which of those who survive are the most like those dearly-remembered objects, and so they fall into a less solemn strain, and become cheerful again.

How many people in all, grandchildren, great-grandchildren, and one or two intimate friends of the family, dine together to-day at the eldest son's to congratulate the old couple, and wish them many happy returns, is a calculation beyond our powers; but this we know, that the old couple no sooner present themselves, very sprucely and carefully attired, than there is a violent shouting and rushing forward of the younger branches with all manner of presents, such as pocket-books, pencil-cases, pen-wipers, watch- papers, pin-cushions, sleeve-buckles, worked-slippers, watch- guards, and even a nutmeg-grater: the latter article being presented by a very chubby and very little boy, who exhibits it in great triumph as an extraordinary variety. The old couple's emotion at these tokens of remembrance occasions quite a pathetic scene, of which the chief ingredients are a vast quantity of kissing and hugging, and repeated wipings of small eyes and noses with small square pocket-handkerchiefs, which don't come at all easily out of small pockets. Even the peevish bachelor is moved, and he says, as he presents the old gentleman with a queer sort of antique ring from his own finger, that he'll be de'ed if he doesn't think he looks younger than he did ten years ago.

But the great time is after dinner, when the dessert and wine are on the table, which is pushed back to make plenty of room, and they are all gathered in a large circle round the fire, for it is then-- the glasses being filled, and everybody ready to drink the toast-- that two great-grandchildren rush out at a given signal, and presently return, dragging in old Jane Adams leaning upon her crutched stick, and trembling with age and pleasure. Who so popular as poor old Jane, nurse and story-teller in ordinary to two generations; and who so happy as she, striving to bend her stiff limbs into a curtsey, while tears of pleasure steal down her withered cheeks!

The old couple sit side by side, and the old time seems like yesterday indeed. Looking back upon the path they have travelled, its dust and ashes disappear; the flowers that withered long ago, show brightly again upon its borders, and they grow young once more in the youth of those about them.

CONCLUSION

We have taken for the subjects of the foregoing moral essays, twelve samples of married couples, carefully selected from a large stock on hand, open to the inspection of all comers. These samples are intended for the benefit of the rising generation of both sexes, and, for their more easy and pleasant information, have been separately ticketed and labelled in the manner they have seen.

We have purposely excluded from consideration the couple in which the lady reigns paramount and supreme, holding such cases to be of a very unnatural kind, and like hideous births and other monstrous deformities, only to be discreetly and sparingly exhibited.

And here our self-imposed task would have ended, but that to those young ladies and gentlemen who are yet revolving singly round the church, awaiting the advent of that time when the mysterious laws of attraction shall draw them towards it in couples, we are desirous of addressing a few last words.

Before marriage and afterwards, let them learn to centre all their hopes of real and lasting happiness in their own fireside; let them cherish the faith that in home, and all the English virtues which the love of home engenders, lies the only true source of domestic felicity; let them believe that round the household gods, contentment and tranquillity cluster in their gentlest and most graceful forms; and that many weary hunters of happiness through the noisy world, have learnt this truth too late, and found a cheerful spirit and a quiet mind only at home at last.

How much may depend on the education of daughters and the conduct of mothers; how much of the brightest part of our old national character may be perpetuated by their wisdom or frittered away by their folly--how much of it may have been lost already, and how much more in danger of vanishing every day--are questions too weighty for discussion here, but well deserving a little serious consideration from all young couples nevertheless.

To that one young couple on whose bright destiny the thoughts of nations are fixed, may the youth of England look, and not in vain, for an example. From that one young couple, blessed and favoured as they are, may they learn that even the glare and glitter of a court, the splendour of a palace, and the pomp and glory of a throne, yield in their power of conferring happiness, to domestic worth and virtue. From that one young couple may they learn that the crown of a great empire, costly and jewelled though it be, gives place in the estimation of a Queen to the plain gold ring that links her woman's nature to that of tens of thousands of her humble subjects, and guards in her woman's heart one secret store of tenderness, whose proudest boast shall be that it knows no Royalty save Nature's own, and no pride of birth but being the child of heaven!

So shall the highest young couple in the land for once hear the truth, when men throw up their caps, and cry with loving shouts -

GOD BLESS THEM.

The Codes Of Hammurabi And Moses
W. W. Davies

QTY

The discovery of the Hammurabi Code is one of the greatest achievements of archaeology, and is of paramount interest, not only to the student of the Bible, but also to all those interested in ancient history...

Religion   **ISBN:** *1-59462-338-4*   **Pages:132**
MSRP $12.95

The Theory of Moral Sentiments
Adam Smith

QTY

This work from 1749. contains original theories of conscience amd moral judgment and it is the foundation for systemof morals.

Philosophy   ISBN: *1-59462-777-0*   **Pages:536**
MSRP $19.95

Jessica's First Prayer
Hesba Stretton

QTY

In a screened and secluded corner of one of the many railway-bridges which span the streets of London there could be seen a few years ago, from five o'clock every morning until half past eight, a tidily set-out coffee-stall, consisting of a trestle and board, upon which stood two large tin cans, with a small fire of charcoal burning under each so as to keep the coffee boiling during the early hours of the morning when the work-people were thronging into the city on their way to their daily toil...

Pages:84

Childrens   ISBN: *1-59462-373-2*   *MSRP $9.95*

My Life and Work
Henry Ford

QTY

Henry Ford revolutionized the world with his implementation of mass production for the Model T automobile. Gain valuable business insight into his life and work with his own auto-biography... "We have only started on our development of our country we have not as yet, with all our talk of wonderful progress, done more than scratch the surface. The progress has been wonderful enough but..."

Pages:300

Biographies/   ISBN: *1-59462-198-5*   *MSRP $21.95*

The Art of Cross-Examination
Francis Wellman

QTY

I presume it is the experience of every author, after his first book is published upon an important subject, to be almost overwhelmed with a wealth of ideas and illustrations which could readily have been included in his book, and which to his own mind, at least, seem to make a second edition inevitable. Such certainly was the case with me; and when the first edition had reached its sixth impression in five months, I rejoiced to learn that it seemed to my publishers that the book had met with a sufficiently favorable reception to justify a second and considerably enlarged edition. ..

Reference   ISBN: *1-59462-647-2*

Pages:412

MSRP $19.95

On the Duty of Civil Disobedience
Henry David Thoreau

QTY

Thoreau wrote his famous essay, On the Duty of Civil Disobedience, as a protest against an unjust but popular war and the immoral but popular institution of slave-owning. He did more than write—he declined to pay his taxes, and was hauled off to gaol in consequence. Who can say how much this refusal of his hastened the end of the war and of slavery ?

Law   ISBN: *1-59462-747-9*

Pages:48

MSRP $7.45

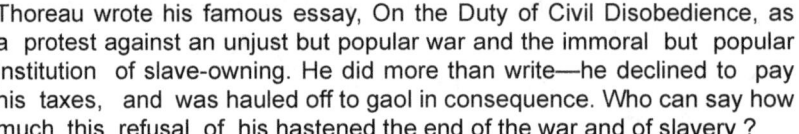

Dream Psychology Psychoanalysis for Beginners
Sigmund Freud

QTY

Sigmund Freud, born Sigismund Schlomo Freud (May 6, 1856 - September 23, 1939), was a Jewish-Austrian neurologist and psychiatrist who co-founded the psychoanalytic school of psychology. Freud is best known for his theories of the unconscious mind, especially involving the mechanism of repression; his redefinition of sexual desire as mobile and directed towards a wide variety of objects; and his therapeutic techniques, especially his understanding of transference in the therapeutic relationship and the presumed value of dreams as sources of insight into unconscious desires.

Psychology   ISBN: *1-59462-905-6*

Pages:196

MSRP $15.45

The Miracle of Right Thought
Orison Swett Marden

QTY

Believe with all of your heart that you will do what you were made to do. When the mind has once formed the habit of holding cheerful, happy, prosperous pictures, it will not be easy to form the opposite habit. It does not matter how improbable or how far away this realization may see, or how dark the prospects may be, if we visualize them as best we can, as vividly as possible, hold tenaciously to them and vigorously struggle to attain them, they will gradually become actualized, realized in the life. But a desire, a longing without endeavor, a yearning abandoned or held indifferently will vanish without realization.

Pages:360

Self Help   ISBN: *1-59462-644-8*

MSRP $25.45

QTY

The Rosicrucian Cosmo-Conception Mystic Christianity by *Max Heindel*　ISBN: *1-59462-188-8*　**$38.95**
The Rosicrucian Cosmo-conception is not dogmatic, neither does it appeal to any other authority than the reason of the student. It is: not controversial, but is: sent forth in the, hope that it may help to clear..　New Age/Religion Pages 646

Abandonment To Divine Providence by *Jean-Pierre de Caussade*　ISBN: *1-59462-228-0*　**$25.95**
"The. Rev. Jean Pierre de Caussade was one of the most remarkable spiritual writers of the Society of Jesus in France in the 18th Century. His death took place at Toulouse in 1751. His works have gone through many editions and have been republished...　Inspirational/Religion Pages 400

Mental Chemistry by *Charles Haanel*　ISBN: *1-59462-192-6*　**$23.95**
Mental Chemistry allows the change of material conditions by combining and appropriately utilizing the power of the mind. Much like applied chemistry creates something new and unique out of careful combinations of chemicals the mastery of mental chemistry...　New Age Pages 354

The Letters of Robert Browning and Elizabeth Barret Barrett 1845-1846 vol II　ISBN: *1-59462-193-4*　**$35.95**
by *Robert Browning* and *Elizabeth Barrett*　Biographies Pages 596

Gleanings In Genesis (volume I) by *Arthur W. Pink*　ISBN: *1-59462-130-6*　**$27.45**
Appropriately has Genesis been termed "the seed plot of the Bible" for in it we have, in germ form, almost all of the great doctrines which are afterwards fully developed in the books of Scripture which follow...　Religion/Inspirational Pages 420

The Master Key by *L. W. de Laurence*　ISBN: *1-59462-001-6*　**$30.95**
In no branch of human knowledge has there been a more lively increase of the spirit of research during the past few years than in the study of Psychology, Concentration and Mental Discipline. The requests for authentic lessons in Thought Control, Mental Discipline and...　New Age/Business Pages 422

The Lesser Key Of Solomon Goetia by *L. W. de Laurence*　ISBN: *1-59462-092-X*　**$9.95**
This translation of the first book of the "Lernegton" which is now for the first time made accessible to students of Talismanic Magic was done, after careful collation and edition, from numerous Ancient Manuscripts in Hebrew, Latin, and French...　New Age/Occult Pages 92

Rubaiyat Of Omar Khayyam by *Edward Fitzgerald*　ISBN:*1-59462-332-5*　**$13.95**
Edward Fitzgerald, whom the world has already learned, in spite of his own efforts to remain within the shadow of anonymity, to look upon as one of the rarest poets of the century, was born at Bredfield, in Suffolk, on the 31st of March, 1809. He was the third son of John Purcell...　Music Pages 172

Ancient Law by *Henry Maine*　ISBN: *1-59462-128-4*　**$29.95**
The chief object of the following pages is to indicate some of the earliest ideas of mankind, as they are reflected in Ancient Law, and to point out the relation of those ideas to modern thought.　Religion/History Pages 452

Far-Away Stories by *William J. Locke*　ISBN: *1-59462-129-2*　**$19.45**
"Good wine needs no bush, but a collection of mixed vintages does. And this book is just such a collection. Some of the stories I do not want to remain buried for ever in the museum files of dead magazine-numbers an author's not unpardonable vanity..."　Fiction Pages 272

Life of David Crockett by *David Crockett*　ISBN: *1-59462-250-7*　**$27.45**
"Colonel David Crockett was one of the most remarkable men of the times in which he lived. Born in humble life, but gifted with a strong will, an indomitable courage, and unremitting perseverance...　Biographies/New Age Pages 424

Lip-Reading by *Edward Nitchie*　ISBN: *1-59462-206-X*　**$25.95**
Edward B. Nitchie, founder of the New York School for the Hard of Hearing, now the Nitchie School of Lip-Reading, Inc, wrote "LIP-READING Principles and Practice". The development and perfecting of this meritorious work on lip-reading was an undertaking...　How-to Pages 400

A Handbook of Suggestive Therapeutics, Applied Hypnotism, Psychic Science　ISBN: *1-59462-214-0*　**$24.95**
by *Henry Munro*　Health/New Age/Health/Self-help Pages 376

A Doll's House: and Two Other Plays by *Henrik Ibsen*　ISBN: *1-59462-112-8*　**$19.95**
Henrik Ibsen created this classic when in revolutionary 1848 Rome. Introducing some striking concepts in playwriting for the realist genre, this play has been studied the world over.　Fiction/Classics/Plays 308

The Light of Asia by *sir Edwin Arnold*　ISBN: *1-59462-204-3*　**$13.95**
In this poetic masterpiece, Edwin Arnold describes the life and teachings of Buddha. The man who was to become known as Buddha to the world was born as Prince Gautama of India but he rejected the worldly riches and abandoned the reigns of power when...　Religion/History/Biographies Pages 170

The Complete Works of Guy de Maupassant by *Guy de Maupassant*　ISBN: *1-59462-157-8*　**$16.95**
"For days and days, nights and nights, I had dreamed of that first kiss which was to consecrate our engagement, and I knew not on what spot I should put my lips..."　Fiction/Classics Pages 240

The Art of Cross-Examination by *Francis L. Wellman*　ISBN: *1-59462-309-0*　**$26.95**
Written by a renowned trial lawyer, Wellman imparts his experience and uses case studies to explain how to use psychology to extract desired information through questioning.　How-to/Science/Reference Pages 408

Answered or Unanswered? by *Louisa Vaughan*　ISBN: *1-59462-248-5*　**$10.95**
Miracles of Faith in China　Religion Pages 112

The Edinburgh Lectures on Mental Science (1909) by *Thomas*　ISBN: *1-59462-008-3*　**$11.95**
This book contains the substance of a course of lectures recently given by the writer in the Queen Street Hail, Edinburgh. Its purpose is to indicate the Natural Principles governing the relation between Mental Action and Material Conditions...　New Age/Psychology Pages 148

Ayesha by *H. Rider Haggard*　ISBN: *1-59462-301-5*　**$24.95**
Verily and indeed it is the unexpected that happens! Probably if there was one person upon the earth from whom the Editor of this, and of a certain previous history, did not expect to hear again...　Classics Pages 380

Ayala's Angel by *Anthony Trollope*　ISBN: *1-59462-352-X*　**$29.95**
The two girls were both pretty, but Lucy who was twenty-one who supposed to be simple and comparatively unattractive, whereas Ayala was credited, as her Bombwhat romantic name might show, with poetic charm and a taste for romance. Ayala when her father died was nineteen...　Fiction Pages 484

The American Commonwealth by *James Bryce*　ISBN: *1-59462-286-8*　**$34.45**
An interpretation of American democratic political theory. It examines political mechanics and society from the perspective of Scotsman James Bryce　Politics Pages 572

Stories of the Pilgrims by *Margaret P. Pumphrey*　ISBN: *1-59462-116-0*　**$17.95**
This book explores pilgrims religious oppression in England as well as their escape to Holland and eventual crossing to America on the Mayflower, and their early days in New England...　History Pages 268

QTY

The Fasting Cure *by Sinclair Upton*   ISBN: *1-59462-222-1*   **$13.95**
In the Cosmopolitan Magazine for May, 1910, and in the Contemporary Review (London) for April, 1910, I published an article dealing with my experiences in fasting. I have written a great many magazine articles, but never one which attracted so much attention... New Age/Self Help/Health Pages 164

Hebrew Astrology *by Sepharial*   ISBN: *1-59462-308-2*   **$13.45**
In these days of advanced thinking it is a matter of common observation that we have left many of the old landmarks behind and that we are now pressing forward to greater heights and to a wider horizon than that which represented the mind-content of our progenitors... Astrology Pages 144

Thought Vibration or The Law of Attraction in the Thought World   ISBN: *1-59462-127-6*   **$12.95**
by William Walker Atkinson   *Psychology/Religion Pages 144*

Optimism *by Helen Keller*   ISBN: *1-59462-108-X*   **$15.95**
Helen Keller was blind, deaf, and mute since 19 months old, yet famously learned how to overcome these handicaps, communicate with the world, and spread her lectures promoting optimism. An inspiring read for everyone... Biographies/Inspirational Pages 84

Sara Crewe *by Frances Burnett*   ISBN: *1-59462-360-0*   **$9.45**
In the first place, Miss Minchin lived in London. Her home was a large, dull, tall one, in a large, dull square, where all the houses were alike, and all the sparrows were alike, and where all the door-knockers made the same heavy sound... Childrens/Classic Pages 88

The Autobiography of Benjamin Franklin *by Benjamin Franklin*   ISBN: *1-59462-135-7*   **$24.95**
The Autobiography of Benjamin Franklin has probably been more extensively read than any other American historical work, and no other book of its kind has had such ups and downs of fortune. Franklin lived for many years in England, where he was agent... Biographies/History Pages 332

Name	
Email	
Telephone	
Address	
City, State ZIP	

☐ **Credit Card**   ☐ **Check / Money Order**

Credit Card Number	
Expiration Date	
Signature	

Please Mail to: Book Jungle
PO Box 2226
Champaign, IL 61825
or Fax to: 630-214-0564

ORDERING INFORMATION

web: *www.bookjungle.com*
email: *sales@bookjungle.com*
fax: *630-214-0564*
mail: *Book Jungle PO Box 2226 Champaign, IL 61825*
or PayPal *to sales@bookjungle.com*

Please contact us for bulk discounts

DIRECT-ORDER TERMS

**20% Discount if You Order
Two or More Books**
Free Domestic Shipping!
Accepted: Master Card, Visa,
Discover, American Express

www.ingramcontent.com/pod-product-compliance
Lightning Source LLC
Chambersburg PA
CBHW081201170626
46813CB00009B/3284